Click It Computer Fun

Geography

By Lisa Trumbauer

The Millbrook Press
Brookfield, Connecticut

Published by The Millbrook Press, Inc., 2 Old New Milford Road, Brookfield, CT 06804.
Printed in the United States of America.

Produced by 17th Street Productions,
a division of Daniel Weiss Associates, Inc.
33 West 17th Street, New York, NY 10011

Cover illustration by Sam Ward
Interior design and illustrations by Sydney Wright

Library of Congress Cataloging-in-Publication Data

Trumbauer, Lisa 1963-
Click it. Computer fun geography / by Lisa Trumbauer ; illustrated by Sydney Wright.
p. cm.
Summary : Explains how to use a personal computer to complete activities that explore various aspects of geography and maps.
ISBN 0-7613-1507-1 (lib. bdg). — ISBN 0-7613-0999-3 (pbk.)
1. Computers—Juvenile literature. 2. Geography—Data processing—Juvenile literature. [1. Computers. 2. Geography—Data processing. 3. Maps—Data processing.] I. Wright, Sydney, 1957- ill.
QA76.23.T77 1999
910' .285'5369—dc21

98-37574
CIP
AC

1 3 5 7 9 10 8 6 4 2

CONTENTS

COOL! A COMPUTER!

Now What?!

What do computers, geography, and fun all have in common? You! When you do the activities in this book, you'll learn all sorts of things about geography by having lots of fun on your computer!

Why Geography?

Geography is a totally cool subject to learn about. What is geography? It's the study of everything, from your house to the whole earth! Every little stream and rock is a part of it, and so are the pyramids, the Grand Canyon, and all the other world wonders. Imagine yourself as a world explorer, discovering the planet. (It is, after all, the place where you live!) As you make the puzzles, mobiles, dioramas, and other projects in this book, you'll discover things you never knew about the earth. Did you know that the continents actually move? Can you understand all the squiggly lines and symbols on a map? And hey—do you know your intergalactic address? What do you think would be the coolest places on earth to visit? And how about making a treasure map—in your own home? It's all part of geography!

But since this is a computer book (duh—you knew that!), you have to know some of the basics first. Here's your computer, inside and out:

What it is: You know that big screen that looks like a TV? That's the **monitor**.
What it does: It shows you what you're working on.

What it is: See all the buttons with letters and numbers on them? They're on the **keyboard.**

What it does: Here's where you type in what you want the computer to do and also all the words you want to appear on the screen.

What it is: Can you find the funky-looking curvy tool with one or two big buttons on it? That's the **mouse.**

What it does: It lets you move around the computer screen and choose where you want to go. How? Simple—once you understand some mouse lingo:

Cursor: This is the blinking line you see on the computer screen. It shows you where you are on the screen. You can move it by moving the mouse.

Click: When the instructions tell you to "click," you push the left button on the mouse and then release it quickly.

Drag: When you need to "drag" the cursor across the screen, you hold down the left button on the mouse and move it across the **mouse pad** it's resting on.

Write On

For the activities in this book, you'll need to understand how to use the **word-processing** program. That's what you use for writing, like when you want to write notes to a friend or make up a story about all your wild adventures as captain of a spaceship. Many different word-processing programs are available, but one of the most popular is **Microsoft Works**. The following activities are based on this program, but you can do them with any other program that your computer has. Here are some tips on how to use **Microsoft Works**:

Click on the word **Start** at the bottom of your computer screen. See that list of words above it? Move your mouse up until the word **Programs** is highlighted, then move your mouse to the right and you'll see the names of all your computer's programs. Look for **Microsoft Works**. Found it? Great! Click on it once, and then you'll see three choices. Click **Works Tools** once and then **Word Processor** once. Easy enough, right? Now you should have a blank screen, just waiting for you to fill it up with your writing!

At the top of the screen you'll see some words. This is called the **Menu Bar.** Move your mouse to one of these words, and an arrow will appear. Click, and you'll get a list with more words, called **commands.** You use them to tell your computer what to do. Here are the commands you will use:

- In **File:** Save, Page Setup, and Print
- In **Edit:** Cut, Copy, and Paste
- In **Insert:** ClipArt, Drawing, and Object
- In **Format:** Font and Style

Below you will see a row of small pictures. This is the **Tool Bar.** The Tool Bar lets you do some things without using a command. For example:

- **Font Box:** This is the first thing you see on the left. It tells you the name of the type style, or font, that you are using. You can choose a new font (**FONT**, font, **font**, *font*) by clicking the arrow to see your choices, then clicking on the one you want.

- **Numbers:** These numbers tell you the size of your type. Click on the arrow to see how large or small you can make the type—small, normal, huge!

- **B I U:** These three boxes let you change the way the type looks.

  B stands for boldface. It makes the type **darker.**
  I stands for italics. It makes the type *slanted.*
  U stands for underline. It draws a line under the type.

- **Lines:** You might see three or four boxes with straight lines in them. These let you move the words you type to different parts of the screen. You can choose to put them all the way to the left, in the middle (centered), all the way to the right, or all lined up on both sides (justified).

Before you begin to type, choose a font and a size. You can do this on the Tool Bar by clicking a new font or type size. You can also do this by clicking **Format,** then clicking **Font and Style.** Here you will see fonts and sizes and **colors!** Choose a color, just as you would a font or a size—by clicking the arrow beside the Color Box to see the choices, then clicking the color once. When you've made all your choices, click the **OK** button to return to the main screen.

Paint Up a Storm

So now you're an expert at the writing stuff. What else is there? Painting! Did you know you could be a master artist without picking up a single paintbrush? You can actually paint pictures on your computer! Since you'll be doing a lot of that in the activities in this book, here's a guide to your **Paint** program:

Click on the word **Start** at the bottom of your screen. Remember this list? Click on **Programs** again, but this time choose the word **Accessories**. Yes, there's *another* list of choices. See the word **Paint**? You guessed it—that's where you click!

Whoa! Look at all your paint tools! And colors! Here's what some of the tools in the **Tool Box** can do:

- Pencil: draws a line
- Paintbrush: paints a thicker line
- Paint Can: fills an object with color
- Spray-Paint Can: makes splotchy, starbursts of color
- "A" Icon: makes a box for you to type words in
- Shapes: these make exact shapes
- Dotted-Line Box: can move or delete art or type
- Eraser: erases color

To change a color, just click the color you want in the **Paint Box**. If you click the Paint Box twice, you'll get a grid with even more colors!

PSST!

Exit the Paint program by clicking the box with the X in the upper right corner.

HINT!

Okay, we know the pictures you paint will be totally amazing, but just in case you want to sneak in some of the stuff by the pros, here's how to do it: **ClipArt**. These are pictures that have already been drawn and are stored inside your computer. In your word-processing program click **Insert**, then **ClipArt**. You'll see pictures of all kinds of things, from flowers to people to computers! Click the arrows to move the list up and down to see them. (This is called **scrolling**.) Then click once on the picture you want. A box will appear around it. Click the **Insert** button. The picture will appear on your word-processing page! The clip art in this book comes from sources other than Microsoft Works, and you can always buy software that contains more clip art!

Now that you know how to write and draw on the computer, there are only two more things to learn before you get started on the *fun* part—the activities! What good would your work be if you couldn't show it off to people? How do you do it? Easy—**save** and **print**.

Saving

Click onto the word **File** at the top of the screen, then click **Save**. Now name your work. Type the name in the white box that says **File Name**. Choose a name you'll remember. Click the **Save** button. Your work has been saved!

Once you've saved your file, you'll want to print it out (see below) or start a new one. Click into **File**, then **New** to start a new page. Your old art will disappear, and a new, clean canvas will take its place. To open the file again, click **File**, then **Open**. Click on the name of your file once, and click the **Open** button again. Your work will appear!

Now Print!

You'll have to print out your "paintings" to put together mobiles, posters, and other projects. It would be best if you had a color printer. If not, don't worry! Follow these steps anyway!

1. Click **File**, then click **Print**.
2. A box with print choices will come on the screen. Some of the activities in this book work better if you choose to print your page in the **Landscape** format. When you need to do that, the instructions will explain how. Otherwise just click **OK**, and your page will print.

That Should Do It!

The activities in this book are based on Windows 95, using Microsoft Works and the Paint program. Many versions of Microsoft Works exist. So you may have to alter the instructions slightly to fit your computer. Also, the pictures show how a finished product *may* look. Don't worry if your art looks a bit different. It probably will! That's because you used *your* ideas and *your* computer!

Computers can do about a billion things, so get ready to see all the fun stuff you can do with your computer. No, it can't clean your room (get serious!), but it lets you try tons of different activities like the ones in this book. Experiment by playing with the pictures, by cutting and pasting, and by choosing fonts, sizes, and colors. Be crazy, be creative, and have a blast!

Chapter One

Out of This World—Not!

Do people ever tell you to start small and work your way up? Well, here's some upside-down logic for you—with geography you start big! What's the biggest thing you can think of? How about the whole galaxy? Pretty gigantic, right? So these activities are all about Earth and the universe around us!

GEOGRAPHY

Stellar Satellite Photo

Geography is all about our home planet, Earth. Close up, the earth is full of trees and other plants, buildings, people, and much more (like the ice-cream shop down the street and that annoying guy in your math class). But when you look at it from far away—like outer space—most of what you see is blue ocean and green land. This is what pictures from cameras in space, on satellites, look like. To get familiar with painting pictures in the Paint program, try painting your own satellite picture.

Steps:

1. Go to your **Paint** program. You'll have a blank canvas, with a **Tool Bar** on one side and rows of colors along the bottom. Click on the **Ellipse tool,** which makes circles and ovals.
2. Choose a color for your Earth by clicking on the color blue in the **Paint Box.** Now click onto the blank canvas. You should see a giant "plus" sign. Hold down the mouse button and **drag** it to form a large circle.
3. Click the **Paint Can,** then click inside the circle to fill it with color.

4 Now draw in the land. Click the **Pencil** (for a thin line) or the **Paintbrush** (for a thicker line). Change the color in the Paint Box to green. Hold down the mouse button and **drag** it through the circle, drawing in the land. Fill the land with color by following step 3. If you make a mistake, use the **Eraser tool** to erase it.

PSST!

To fill something with color, all the lines need to be connected to make an enclosed space. If you fill your land with color and the entire Earth fills up, then you have an open line somewhere. Don't panic! Click Edit, then click Undo. The color will disappear. Find where the line is open using the magnifier tool on your tool bar, then click the Pencil, close it up, and fill with color again.

5 **Save** and **Print** your work!

COOL IDEA!

If you were really taking pictures of Earth from a satellite, it would be covered with white swirling clouds. Try the Spray-Paint Can and white paint to cover your world with clouds.

GEOGRAPHY

Get My Drift?

Can you feel the ground move? Probably not. But it does! The earth is made up of seven large pieces of land called continents. (These were the big blobs of land you drew on your picture of Earth.) Millions and millions of years ago the continents were joined together in one supercontinent called Pangaea. Slowly they broke apart and drifted away from each other. This is called continental drift. And the continents are still drifting—about one inch a year! If you look at the continents today, you can see how they might have been joined long, long ago, like pieces of a puzzle. Make your own supercontinent puzzle that you can take apart and put back together.

Steps:

1 Go into your **Paint** program. Click on the **Pencil tool,** and draw the outline of a large continent.

2 Then draw lines through the continent, as if it is cracked and about to break apart. Now you have seven puzzle pieces. Using the **Paint Can** and other **Paint tools,** fill in each piece with a different color. You can even draw patterns in them if you want!

PSST!

Your art will print better if it is set for landscape. Click File, Page Setup. Look for the word *orientation.* Click landscape, then OK.

3 **Save** your art and **print** it out.

4 Glue your art to a thin piece of cardboard or poster board. Cut apart the pieces along the lines you drew.

5 Put the puzzle pieces together to form your supercontinent again! Let a friend try it too!

CONTINENTS

North America South America Africa Europe
Asia Australia Antarctica

GEOGRAPHY

Calling All Earthlings!

Special message from outer space! Of course, you know your address—that's how you get mail from people on Earth. But what if you could get mail from outer space? You would need to know more information than just your street or your city for an intergalactic address. You'd have to find out what continent you live on and which hemisphere you're in. That means learning more geography! Check your atlas or globe to get all the necessary info. Then you can make a cool banner to hang on your wall that could show any alien how to find you!

Steps:

1. Go into the **Paint** program. Paint a spaceship or a flying saucer. Add some alien creatures or anything you can think of that might be in space!
2. Add outer-space color to the background. Click the **Paint Can,** then choose black from the **Paint Box.** Move the cursor outside the spaceship and click. Add star bursts by clicking the **Spray-Paint Can** and a yellow color.
3. Now type in your address. Click the **A icon.** Place the cursor on the art, hold down the mouse button, and drag it to make a text box. Type in your name.
4. **Save** your art and **print** it out.
5. To erase the type, click the **Dotted-Line Box** at the top of the **Tool Bar.** Drag it over the type so a box forms around it. Press the **Delete** key on the keyboard. It's gone!
6. Fill in the color again, using the **Paint Can.**
7. Now make a new text box and type in the next part of your address. **Print.**
8. Follow steps 3 through 7 to make all the parts of your address.
9. Tape the pages together, in address order, to make an intergalactic wall banner!

PSST!

Don't forget to use the shape and line tools!

Chapter Two

BY LAND AND SEA

You're set with the planet now, right?
The next step in learning about geography is knowing all about the things on the earth. Yeah, that could be anything from you to your TV, but then it wouldn't be geography anymore!
These activities are all about major monuments and natural creations from all over the world.

GEOGRAPHY

HOLY MOLEHILL!

A mountain is totally different from an ocean, right? Well, yeah, it is, but mountains and oceans are both types of *landforms*. Landforms are all the features of nature that make up our earth, like rivers, glaciers, and islands too! Here's how to make a mobile (a decoration with hanging pieces of art attached by strings) that you can hang up to show all the different landforms.

Steps:

1 Go into the **Paint** program. Experiment with the paint tools to draw and paint landforms, like the ones listed here.

Landforms

valleys	islands	peninsulas	glaciers
mountains	plateaus	buttes	canyons
caves	hills	rivers	lakes
volcanoes	oceans	waterfalls	icebergs
plains	bays	gorges	

HINT! If your canvas is small, click the box in the upper-righthand corner that has one square in it. This will make the canvas bigger!

2 Save your landforms, and print them out. Cut out each landform too.

3 Now you will need a paper plate, scissors, some string, and tape. First poke a hole in the center of the plate. Cut lengths of string—one for each landform and one to hang up the mobile. Thread one string through the hole in the plate and knot it so it won't slip out. Now tape one end of a string to each landform and the other end to the plate rim. Make sure the landforms are evenly spaced around the plate. Your mobile is ready for hanging!

HINT!

You don't need to paint all your landforms on the same canvas. Start a new painting for each one! Save your work, then click File, New. A new, blank canvas will pop up.

COOL IDEA!

Make some mega-landforms, like these below—the tallest, longest, and biggest landforms on our planet!

MEGA LANDFORMS

The Tallest Mountain:	Mount Everest, Nepal and Tibet	29,028 feet!
The Longest River:	The Nile, Egypt and Sudan	4,160 miles!
The Biggest Desert:	The Sahara, Africa	3,500,000 square miles!
The Tallest Waterfall:	Angel Falls, Venezuela	3,212 feet!
The Biggest Island:	Greenland	840,000 square miles!
The Deepest Ocean:	The Pacific Ocean	12,925 feet!
The Biggest Continent:	Asia	17,400,000 square miles!
The Biggest Lake:	Caspian Sea, in Europe and Asia	43,244 square miles!

*Statistics found in the *World Almanac for Kids 1998, World Almanac Books,* a K-III Communications Company (Mahwah, N.J.: 1997).

GEOGRAPHY

WHO MADE THIS?

Everything on our planet can be divided into two categories—things made by people or things made by nature. For example, the Grand Canyon was definitely made by nature. But the faces on Mount Rushmore were made by people. Make a *collage* (that's a fancy art term for a bunch of pictures stuck together) to show these two features of our planet.

Steps:

1 Think of famous people-made features that you think are pretty amazing, like the Statue of Liberty, Mayan pyramids, or your city's baseball stadium. While in your **word-processing** program, flip through the clip art and choose pictures of human-made things. Insert each piece of art onto its own page. Make each piece of art as big as possible, save, then print it out.

2 Now think of all the natural features you know, like Niagara Falls, the Mississippi River, or the Rocky Mountains. Again, scroll through your clip art to find pictures of them. They can be specific ones or general scenes, like a forest, a lake, or an iceberg. Insert each piece of art onto its own page. Make the art as big as possible, then save and print it out.

3 Write a heading for each column: "Made by People" and "Made by Nature." (You could create these headings on the computer too, choosing a font, a color, and a large type size, then printing.)

PSST!

If clip art isn't available, draw the features using the Paint program.

4 Cut out all the art. Now get a sheet of poster board. Divide it in half by drawing a line down the center or by gluing a strip of construction paper down the center.

5 Now arrange your pictures however you want, keeping the ones that show things made by people separate from the ones that show things made by nature. When you like your collage, glue down the art.

6 Hang your poster in your bedroom, your kitchen, or wherever you want it!

Chapter Three

Zoning Out

Your room is one of your favorite places to be because everything there is perfect for you, right? Your favorite music playing and your coolest posters on the walls? Well, all over the world creatures have their own places that are perfect for them because of the temperature (hot or cold), the weather (dry or rainy), and lots of other reasons. These places are called habitats, and here are a couple of activities where you can create your own!

GEOGRAPHY

Animal Zone

What can be hot or cold with animals all over? Animal habitats! They can be found all over the world—from dry deserts to the deepest oceans to the snowy polar regions. Penguins live in cold habitats, and lizards live in hot ones. And habitats can be made up of many different landforms (remember landforms? Lakes, rivers, caves, hills, and all the others . . .). So habitats are part of geography! Pick your favorite animal, then make your own animal habitat in a diorama—a three-dimensional scene in a shoe box.

Steps:

1 Choose the habitat you want to make. The box on this page will give you some ideas. Then find a shoe box.

Animal Habitats

coral reef	ocean
pond	swamp
rain forest	desert
tundra	forest
grasslands	mountains
North or South pole	prairie

2 Now draw the background for the diorama. Go into your **Paint** program. Using the **Paint tools,** draw a picture of the habitat.

3 **Save** your scene and **print** it out.

PSST!

Make sure the page is set for landscape! (Click File, then Page Setup.)

4 Click **File,** then click **New** to get a new canvas. Create more pieces of art for the diorama. You can make trees, flowers, grass, animals, rocks, and other cool things that are found in this habitat. Don't forget to save each piece and print it out. Next, cut out the pictures.

5 Glue the art on the inside—and, if you want, to the outside—of your shoe box. Or, tape paper tabs to the bottom so they can stand on the diorama floor.

COOL IDEA!

Make your animal roam your diorama scene. Draw the animal on the computer, or use clip art. (See below.) Save your animal and print it out. Cut out the animal, and tape a pencil or straw to the back. Cut a slit in the top of the shoe box. Slip the animal through the slit and move it through the habitat!

PSST!

You can use clip art for the animals too!

PEOPLE ZONE

GEOGRAPHY

Now you know about animal habitats. But did you know that people live in habitats too? That's right. Everything around you—the houses, the people, the stores and mail-boxes—they're all a part of your habitat! Your neighbor-hood is your habitat. Make a 3-D picture of the street your house is on, with all the other houses and things nearby in it!

Steps:

1. Go into the **Paint** program. Click on the **Pencil tool,** and draw your street. Include turns and other streets that cross it.

2. Click on the **A icon.** Move the cursor to the middle of your street. Hold down the mouse button, and drag the mouse to create a text box within the street. Now type in the street name.

3. Click on the **Paintbrush** and draw your house. Remember to change colors. Add trees and other features. Just for fun, put in all the things you wish your street had too, like a candy store open all night or a zoo full of wonderful animals. Use your imagination, and make the habitat you'd feel most at home in!

4. Now **save** your art and **print** it out. Take your picture outside and try to follow it to see if you've drawn your street cor-rectly.

5. Glue your street to a piece of poster board. Fold the poster board in half, where your street meets your house. Prop it up on a bookshelf. Place model cars on your street.

PSST!

Make sure the page is set for landscape! (Click File, then Page Setup.)

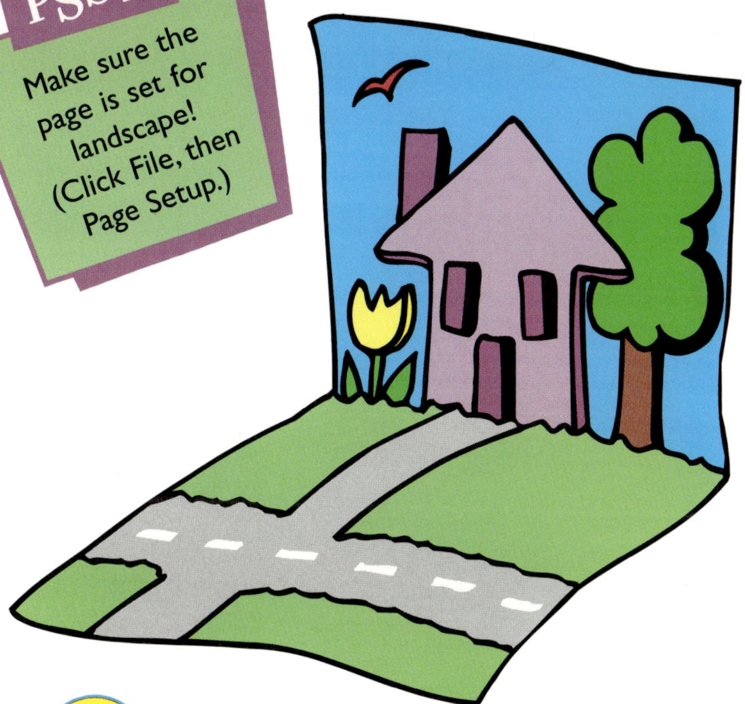

Chapter Four

Sign Language

Remember when you were little and your street used to look gigantic to you? Now you know about the rest of the world and the whole universe, so your neighborhood doesn't seem that big anymore. But all the signs and other road rules are actually pretty important for geography because they help you know how to get places and what you can do when you're there. Here are a couple of activities to get you familiar with road signs and rules!

GEOGRAPHY First AsSIGNment

Stop! Go! Don't Walk! Deer X-ing! **These are messages we read on signs. Signs tell you all kinds of information about where you are and what you can and can't do in different places. Do you want to be the boss of what people can do in your room? Make some signs to hang on your door and walls, and be as wacky as you want!**

Steps:

1 Go into the **Paint** program. Click on the **Rectangle tool,** and draw a large rectangular box. Click the **Paint Can,** and fill the sign with any color you want.

2 Then click the **Paintbrush,** and choose a thick line. Think about what people should know before they enter your room—"Enter at Your Own Risk!" "Disaster Area!" "Keep Quiet—Genius at Work!" Choose a color, and paint your message on your sign.

PSST! The box below the tools shows you the thickness your Paintbrush and Spray Paint can be.

3 Save your sign, and **print** it out.

4 Make other signs the same way. Remember, you don't always have to use the rectangle—you can also use a circle, a triangle, or any shape you want!

5 Back your signs with poster board or cardboard to make them sturdy, then hang the signs around your room.

PSST!

Make sure the page is set for landscape! (Click File, then Page Setup.)

HINT!

To erase a letter you painted within your sign, use the Paint Can instead of the Eraser tool. Choose the color of your sign, then fill in the letter with paint. Click back onto the Paintbrush, change the color back to the one you were using to paint your letter, then write it again.

GEOGRAPHY

Radical Roads

Following roads and reading signs are geography skills. You probably use them all the time when you ride your bike or ride in a car. Now that you know how to make signs and draw streets, you can make a whole model town in your room!

Steps:

1 First clear an area in your room for your roads. It can be on the floor, on a desk, on a bookshelf, or wherever you think you have enough space.

2 Follow the directions on page 20 to make road signs—but be sure to make these signs small. Now make each sign stand up. Tape a craft stick, a straw, or a toothpick to the back, then cut a hole in an empty box (like a ring box). Put the stick through the hole, and your sign will stand on its own!

3 Now make roads. You should still be in your **Paint** program. Click on a thick **Paintbrush,** and draw lines for a road. Make a dotted line in the center to show how the road divides. **Save** your road. **Print** out lots of copies.

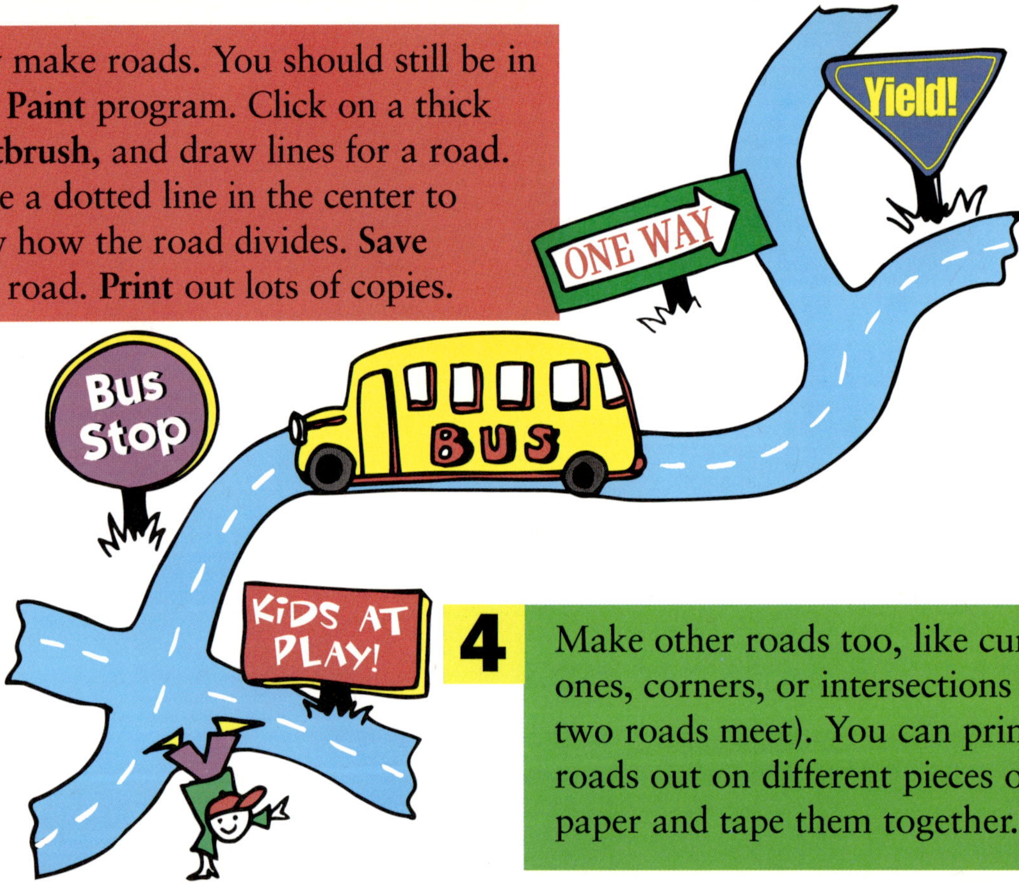

4 Make other roads too, like curvy ones, corners, or intersections (where two roads meet). You can print the roads out on different pieces of paper and tape them together.

5 Now set up your roads in your cleared space. Line up the roads so that you have long ones, short ones, and crossing ones.

6 Place your road signs along the side of the roads.

7 To make your town look even more realistic and fun, add some places to go and things to do there! In the Paint program paint the fronts of stores, homes, and other cool spots like a movie theater. Save, print, and cut them out. Glue the pictures to small cereal boxes to add these buildings along your roads!

8 Now move model cars, miniature animals or people, and other fun stuff around in your model town!

Chapter Five

Map Mysteries

Since geography is all about places (you certainly know that by now!), knowing how to read a map is a huge help so that you can always find your way around. But sometimes maps can be pretty confusing. These next activities will show you what all those little symbols mean, and turn you into a map expert in no time!

GEOGRAPHY

WHICH WAY IS UP?

North, south, east, and west. These are the four main directions. A compass can tell you which direction you're headed in, and that's important when you're hiking, biking, or even riding in a car. A magnetic compass has a needle or an arrow that always points to the North Pole no matter which way you turn it. This way you always know where north is. And if you know where north is, you can figure out which way south, east, and west are! A compass rose on a map is like a picture of a compass. It shows you which way is north too. Make your own compass rose to hang on your window.

Steps:

1. Go into the **Paint** program. Draw a large circle. This will be the base for your compass rose.

2. Click the **Straight-Line tool,** and draw 4 triangles outside the circle—at the top, bottom, left, and right. Fill in the 4 triangles with color by clicking the **Paint Can,** choosing a color, and then clicking into each triangle.

3 To add text, click the **A icon,** then click white in your **Paint Box.** Set up the text box, and type in the letter for each direction: N, S, E, and W.

PSST!

If you make a mistake, click Edit, then Undo, and your mistake will disappear!

4 Make a design in your circle. Experiment with the different **Paint** tools and colors.

5 **Save,** then **print** out your compass rose. (The Landscape format will probably work best.)

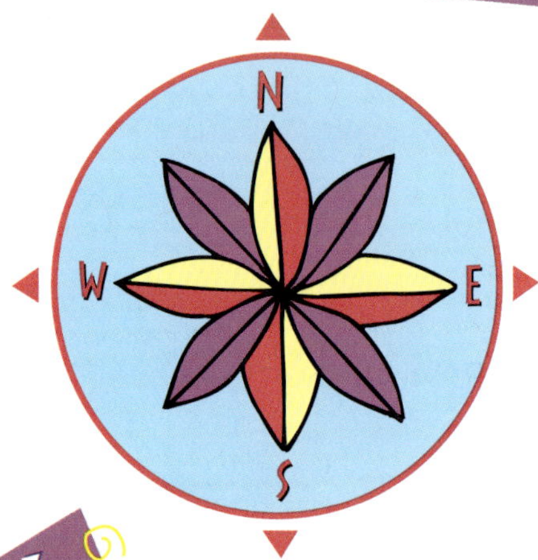

6 Poke a hole in the top point, and thread some string through. Hang your compass rose in a window.

7 Use a real compass to find out which way is north. Move your paper compass so it points this way too!

HINT!

To make your compass rose more sturdy, trace it onto poster board. Cut out the poster-board shape, then glue your compass rose to it.

GEOGRAPHY

CRACK THE CODE!

A compass rose is one picture you'll see on a map, but there are lots of others, like strange lines and symbols. What do they mean? That's what the map key, or *legend,* is for! It breaks the map code by telling you what each picture means. Make your own map legend to learn some basic map symbols, and create some of your own symbols too!

Steps:

1 Go into the **Paint** program. Click on the **Rectangle tool,** and draw a large box. This will be the outline of your map legend.

2 Click the **Straight-Line tool,** and draw a line a little bit down from the top and stretch it across the width of the box. Click the **A icon** to place a title in the top box. Type the heading "Map Legend." Use the **Space Bar** to position the words.

3 Place the cursor under the line you drew. Then on the left side of the legend draw a symbol from a real map. You can use either the **Pencil** or the **Paintbrush.** If you choose the Paintbrush, be sure to choose a thickness in the box below the **Paint tools.**

4 Then type what the symbol means on the right side of the legend. Click the **A icon** to set up the text box.

5 Add as many symbols as will fit. Draw symbols that you think look cool, and then make up meanings for them. Create new legends when you run out of room!

6 **Save** your legend, and **print** it out.

HINT!

Once you draw art or type in a word, you can move it around. Click the Dotted-Line Box at the top of the Tool Bar. Starting at the top-left corner of the art or word, hold down the mouse button and drag it over the art or word so that it is enclosed in a dotted box. Release the mouse button. Now move your cursor inside the box. You will get a thick, dark cross. Hold down the mouse button, and move the art or words by moving the mouse!

GEOGRAPHY

X MARKS THE SPOT

Of course, when you think of treasure maps, you probably imagine desert islands, pirates, and chests full of gold. Create an ancient-looking treasure map for an imaginary island, and make up a story to go with it. Then send it out to sea!

Steps:

1 Go into the **Paint** program. Click the **Paintbrush.** Choose a thick line and a light green color. Draw an outline for your island. Click the **Paint Can** to fill it in.

2 Now draw cool stuff on your island. With a thick **Paintbrush** and brown paint, draw mountains. Choose dark blue to make rivers. The **Spray-Paint**

Can in yellow makes sandy beaches. But since it's your island, you can put whatever you want on it! Play with the different colors and tools to make your island look as you want it to—with all your favorite things, like palm trees, boats, fish, or even pirates.

3 Switching back to the **Paintbrush** in black, create a dotted line across the island, leading to the buried treasure. Draw an X to show where it is.

4 To surround the island with a light blue ocean, click the **Paint Can**. Choose the color, then move the cursor outside the island. When you click, the rest of the map will fill with color.

5 **Save** your map. Make sure you've selected **Landscape**, then **print** it out.

HINT!

To see your map before you print it, click File, then Print Preview. Click Close to exit.

Here's how to make your map extra-official, just like a real buried treasure map:

- Make your map look very old. Blot it with a damp sponge so it is slightly wet. Place the map on a windowsill to dry. The dried map will look old and crinkly! Cut some jagged edges for a finishing touch!
- Imagine you found this treasure map in your backyard. Think up a cool story to tell about it. Type your story in your **word-processing** program.
- Send your map in a bottle! First write a note on the back of the map, asking whomever finds it to write where they found it and to mail it back. Then roll up your map and place it in a plastic bottle. Write your name and address on an envelope, put a stamp on the envelope, and put it in the bottle too. Secure the bottle cap tightly. Toss the bottle into a nearby stream. See where your map ends up when someone mails it back!

Chapter Six

TRAVEL MANIA

Geography is also all about the fabulous and exciting places in the world. Pretend you're a world traveler for these activities and make the photo album, postcards, and passport that will help you on your journeys!

GEOGRAPHY

AWESOME ALBUMS

Our planet is full of great places to see and learn about. There are beautiful islands and amazing creations, like pyramids and castles. If you could travel the world and discover the coolest spots, where would *you* go? Start a photo album of places you'd like to see.

Pages with Paintings

Steps:

1 Using the **Paint** program, paint pictures of any places you want to put in your album, from that beach you went to with your family when you were little, to a city in Europe you've always wanted to visit.

2 After you **save** each picture, click **Edit**, then **Select All**. Then click **Edit** again, and this time click **Copy**.

3 **Exit** the **Paint** program. Now open a **word-processing** document.

4 Go into **Edit**, and click **Paste**. Like magic, your picture should appear!

5 Click on your picture so a box forms around it. See the dots on the box? They let you change the size of the art. Try it! Move the cursor over a dot until you see the word Resize. Then hold down the mouse button, and drag the mouse. Experiment to get the size you want.

6 Click outside the art box, on the right side of it, and hit the **Return** key. This will move the cursor below the art. Now write about your cool place. Explain what it is, where it is found, and any other fun facts you learn.

7 Make a heading for your page too. Click into the **Header** box at the top of the page. Click **Format**, then **Font** and **Style**. Here, choose a font (type style), size, and color for your title. Click on each one you want, then click **OK**. You'll return to the header box. Begin to type! To center the title, click the box on the tool bar with the lines in the middle.

8 **Save** your photo-album page, and **print** it out. Then make more, repeating the above steps.

Pages with Clip Art

Don't forget! Your computer already comes with some art—clip art! Try some clip art for your photo pages.

Steps:

1 Paint a vertical or a horizontal border in the **Paint** program, or find some border art in your clip art. Follow the directions on pages 27-28 for inserting it onto a word-processing page.

2 Move your borders as close as possible to the edge of the paper by changing the margins. Click **File, Page Setup**. Under **Margins**, change the measurements to .5 for each. Click **OK**. Your borders will move closer to the edge of the page.

Album Cover

You can use the skills you've learned to paint a cover for your photo album.

3 Type a title in the center of your page. Make it big and colorful! (Go into **Format, Font,** and **Style** to change the font, size, and color.)

4 Before you print, check **Print Preview** (under **File**). Do you like your cover? Is the title the right size? Is the art in the right places? If so, **print** it out! Don't forget to **save** your cover too.

construction paper

Put It All Together!

Cut sheets of construction paper slightly bigger than your album pages. Glue each page to a sheet of construction paper, using both the front and the back. Add extra, blank pages of construction paper. Staple all the pages together, with the cover on the front. Each time you make a new album page, glue it to a blank construction-paper page.

GEOGRAPHY

WISH YOU WERE HERE!

Have you ever gotten a postcard from someone on vacation? On one side you saw an awesome picture of a place. And on the other side was a note from your friend. Make a postcard to send to someone else, with a picture of a place you've been to—or want to go to someday—and then write your own personal message!

Steps:

1 Open up the **word-processing** program. Click **Insert, ClipArt** to view your clip-art choices. Look for pictures of deserts or islands or any other kinds of places you like. If you don't have clip art for the places you've been, draw pictures of them yourself in the **Paint** program.

2 **Insert** the clip art or **paste** your painting into a word-processing document. Make the picture as wide as it can be, and have it fill about half the page. This is the front of the postcard.

PSST!

Remember—the clip art in this book is from sources other than Microsoft Works!

3 Now make the back. Click outside your art, and hit the **Return** key several times. Go under **Format**, and click **Borders** and **Shading**. Choose a thickness and click. A box with a border will appear below your picture! You should see the cursor blinking inside the box too. Make the box bigger by hitting the **Return** key. Your picture and your box should be about the same size. (Click **File, Print Preview** to check.)

4 Now start typing. First write a sentence explaining what the picture you drew on the front of the postcard is. Then add writing lines for your message. (Hold down the **Shift** key, and hit the **Dash** key, between 0 and =.) Make the lines go only halfway across the page. Leave the other half blank so you can write the person's address.

5 **Save** and **print** your postcard.

6 Cut out the postcard pieces, then glue them together back to back. For sturdier postcards glue them to poster board.

7 Write a message that explains why you think this would be a cool place to visit and what you would do there. Mail your postcard to a friend or someone in your family.

GEOGRAPHY "PASSPORT, PLEASE"

That's what you'll hear if you travel to a different country. Your passport is an official document that looks like a little book. It tells what country you are from. Each time you travel to a new country, you get a stamp in your passport. Make your own passport to collect stamps in!

Steps:

1 Go into the **Paint** program. Start with the **Rectangle tool.** Create the outline of your passport by making a large rectangle shape.

2 Divide the rectangle in half. Click the **Straight-Line tool,** and draw a line from the top of the rectangle down to the bottom.

3 Make the passport cover on the right side of the rectangle. You'll use the left half of the rectangle for the back cover. With the **A icon** and the other **Paint tools,** make an official-looking seal and write the word "Passport."

4 **Save** it with the name "Passport Cover," then **print** it out.

5 Now click **File, Save As.** Rename the card "Passport Inside." This way you don't have to make a new rectangle base. (This rectangle needs to be the same as the "cover" rectangle.) Delete the art and text on the card. Click the **Dotted-Line Box,** and drag it over the art and text until it is all enclosed in the dotted box. Then hit the **Delete** key on the keyboard. Do the same for the other side. Your passport should now be empty.

6 On the left side of the passport, draw a picture of yourself. Leave the right side blank.

7 **Save** and **print** out the inside of the passport.

8 Cut out both pictures. Glue or glue-stick them back to back. Fold the card in half so the cover is on the outside. Stamp the inside of the passport with stamps you already have, or draw stamps on the computer to glue inside.